SUPER BOWL
WASHINGTON REDSKINS
CHAMPIONS

SUPER BOWL

Published by Creative Education
123 South Broad Street
Mankato, Minnesota 56001
Creative Education is an imprint of The Creative Company.

DESIGN AND PRODUCTION BY **EVANSDAY DESIGN**

LIBRARY OF CONGRESS CATALOGING-IN-PUBLICATION DATA

LeBoutillier, Nate.
Washington Redskins / Nate LeBoutillier.
p. cm. — (Super Bowl champions)
Includes index.
ISBN 978-1-58341-392-0
1. Washington Redskins (Football team)—Juvenile literature. I. Title.

GV956.W3 L43 2005
796.332'6409753—dc22   2005929760

9 8 7 6

COVER PHOTO: running back Clinton Portis

PHOTOGRAPHS BY

AP/Wide World Photos, Corbis (Bettmann, Wally McNamee), Getty Images (Allsport, Al Bello, David Stluka), Icon Sports Media Inc., SportsChrome USA

CHAMPIONS

WASHINGTON REDSKINS

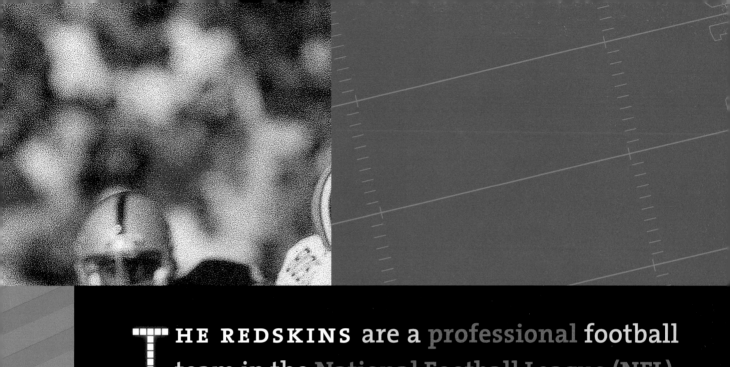

THE REDSKINS are a professional football team in the National Football League (NFL). They play in Washington, D.C. Washington is the capital of the United States.

The Redskins started playing football more than 70 years ago ^

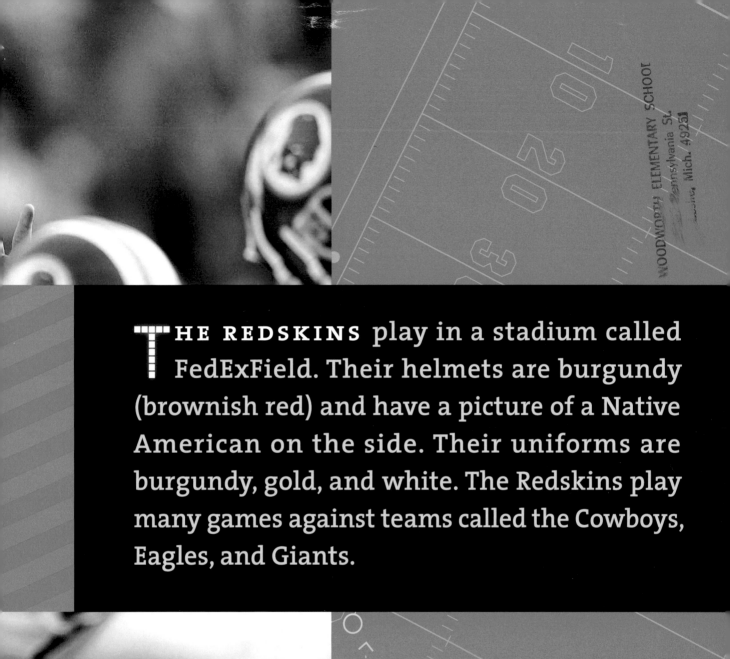

THE REDSKINS play in a stadium called FedExField. Their helmets are burgundy (brownish red) and have a picture of a Native American on the side. Their uniforms are burgundy, gold, and white. The Redskins play many games against teams called the Cowboys, Eagles, and Giants.

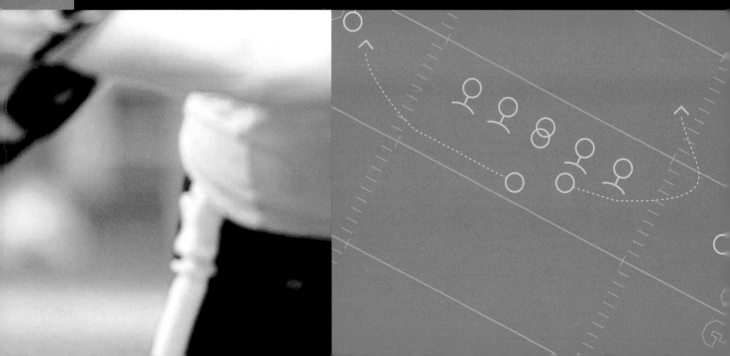

THE REDSKINS played their first season in 1932. At first they played in Boston, Massachusetts. They were named the Braves then. They were re-named the Redskins the next year. In 1937, they moved to Washington. The Redskins won the NFL championship in 1937 and 1942.

The Redskins had very different uniforms in the 1930s ^

Sammy Baugh ran fast and could throw long passes ^

SAMMY BAUGH (*Bah*) was the Redskins' first great player. He played quarterback, running back, and punter. Sometimes he played defense, too. Fans called him "Slingin' Sammy." He is in the NFL Hall of Fame.

Sonny Jurgensen was a good Redskins quarterback ^

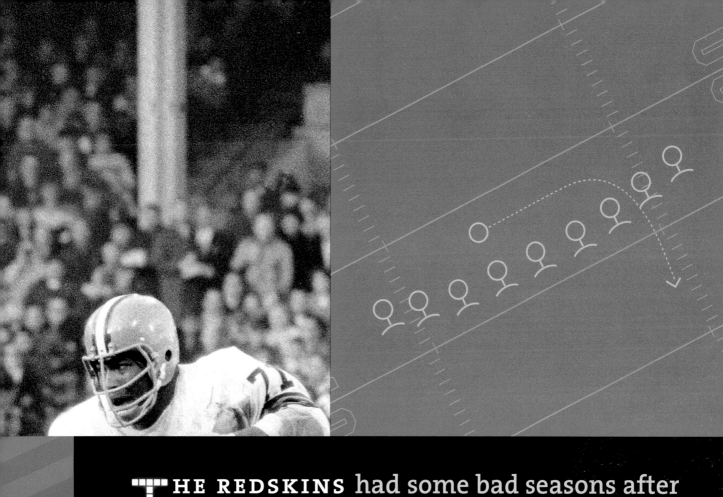

THE REDSKINS had some bad seasons after Sammy Baugh retired. Once they lost a game 73–0! It took a long time for the Redskins to become a good team again.

John Riggins was a star running back for Coach Gibbs ^

IN 1981, the Redskins got a new coach named Joe Gibbs. He helped the Redskins go to three Super Bowls. The Redskins won the Super Bowl all three times—in 1982, 1987, and 1991.

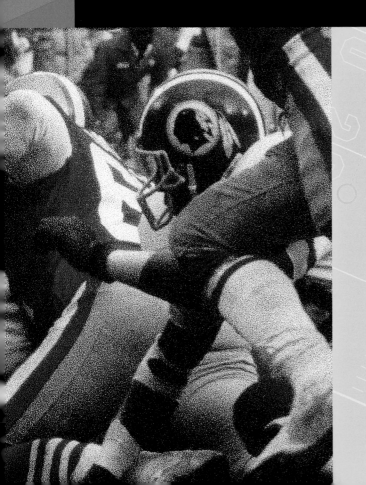

JOE THEISMANN (*Thyz-men*) played quarterback for the Redskins. He was a good passer and handed the ball off to John Riggins. John was not very fast, but he was tough. He liked to run over players.

Joe Theismann helped his team win the 1982 Super Bowl

Darrell Green stole lots of passes from other teams ^

DARRELL GREEN played cornerback. He was one of the fastest players ever. He played for the Redskins for 20 seasons. That is the longest anyone has ever played for one NFL team.

TODAY, THE Redskins have a tough defense. LaVar Arrington is one of their best players. He is a linebacker who tackles hard. Redskins fans hope that he will help lead the team back to the Super Bowl!

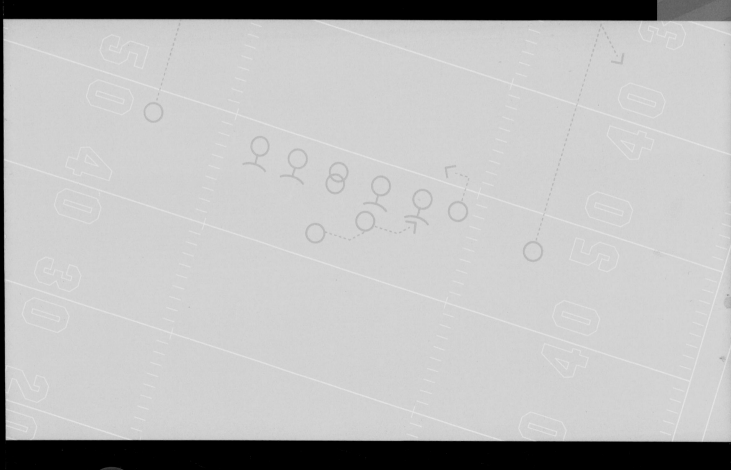

Strong linebacker LaVar Arrington was hard to block

GLOSSARY

capital

the city where the laws for a state or country are made

Hall of Fame

a club that only the best NFL players and coaches
get to join

National Football League (NFL)

a group of football teams that play against each other;
there are 32 teams in the NFL today

professional

a person or team that gets paid to play or work

retired

stopped playing or working for good

FUN FACTS

Team colors
Burgundy, gold, and white

Home stadium
FedExField (86,484 seats)

Conference/Division
National Football Conference (NFC), East Division

First season
1932

Super Bowl wins
1982 (beat Miami Dolphins 27–17)
1987 (beat Denver Broncos 42–10)
1991 (beat Buffalo Bills 37–24)

Training camp location
Ashburn, Virginia

NFL Web site for kids
http://www.playfootball.com

INDEX